# MOG
## and the Baby

written and illustrated by
# Judith Kerr

HarperCollins *Children's Books*

*For Ben Davis,
who is very fond of cats*

## Picture books by Judith Kerr

First published in hardback in Great Britain by William Collins Sons & Co Ltd in 1980. First published in paperback by Picture Lions in 1982. This edition published by HarperCollins Children's Books in 2005

21

ISBN: 978-0-00-717132-3

Visit our website at: www.harpercollins.co.uk

Printed and bound in China

One day Mog was playing with Nicky.

Debbie was going to school.
Mr Thomas was going to work,
but Nicky had a cold.

Mog and Nicky played
Catch the String.

Then they played Bad Dogs.

Then they played Tickle Mog's Tummy,

and then they played ball.

Suddenly they heard a noise.
It was a crying noise.
It was a very loud crying noise.

Mrs Thomas said, "Look who's here.
Mrs Clutterbuck has brought us her baby.
We're going to look after it while she goes shopping."

The baby looked at Mog
and stopped crying.
It said Psss instead.

"It's trying to say puss,"
said Mrs Thomas.

"Will my baby be all
right with your cat?"
said Mrs Clutterbuck.

"Oh yes," said Mrs Thomas.
"Mog loves babies."

But Mog and Nicky had to stop playing ball
because the baby did not know how to play.

"I've got a very good idea,"
said Mrs Thomas. "Let's take
the baby for a ride in the pram."

The baby liked riding in the pram.
It said Psss.
"I've got a baby in a pram too," said Nicky.
Mog said nothing, but she was not happy.

When they came back it was lunch time.
But the baby did not want to eat its lunch.
It said Psss instead.

It said Psss and cried.
It cried so much that Mog did not
want to eat her lunch either.

She went away
and sat in her basket.

She sat in her basket
and tried to think of
other things, while
Mrs Thomas and Nicky
cleared the dishes.

The baby found a dish
to clear, too.

"Look what it's done," said Nicky.

"Oh dear,"
said Mrs Thomas.
"Perhaps the baby
would like a rest."

But the baby did
not want a rest.
It said Psss Psss Psss.
It said Psss and cried.

"It wants Mog,"
said Mrs Thomas.

"Will Mog be all right
with the baby?" said Nicky.

"Oh yes," said Mrs Thomas, "Mog loves babies."

Mog sat in her basket, and the baby stopped crying.
It was nice and quiet when the baby stopped crying.
It was so quiet that Mog fell asleep.

She had a dream.
It was a lovely dream.
It was a dream about babies.

SUDDENLY... she woke up.

Mog thought,
this baby is everywhere.

She thought,
I'm getting out.

Mog ran across the road,

but the baby was coming after her,

and a bad dog was waiting
on the other side,

and there was a car coming.

"There's my baby!" shouted Mrs Clutterbuck.
"There's Mog!" shouted Debbie.
There's only one way to go,
thought Mog, and she jumped.
She jumped away from the dog.
She jumped away from the car.
She bumped into the baby.
The baby flew through the air
and came down on the pavement.
It said Psss.
Mr Thomas stopped the car just in time.

"My baby! Oh, my baby!" said Mrs Clutterbuck.

"It's a silly baby," said Nicky.

"It shouldn't have run into the road."

"Mog saved it," said Debbie.

"She is a very brave cat," said Nicky.

"She is the bravest cat in the world. She is a
baby-saving cat, and she should have a reward."

They all went to get Mog a reward.
It was a very big reward.
It was a reward from Mrs Clutterbuck.

"Mog saved my baby from being run over,"
said Mrs Clutterbuck.
"I told you," said Mrs Thomas, "Mog loves babies."